Martin Bridge
Blazing Ahead!

Written by
Jessica Scott Kerrin

Illustrated by
Joseph Kelly

Kids Can Press

For Peter and Elliott. And for my sister Leslie,
the real camper of the family — J.S.K.

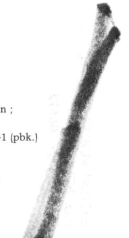

For my dad Joe, the snappiest dancer in the USN, who
really has seen manta rays, circular rainbows and a chocolate
river called the Orinoco, all from the pilot seat of a blimp! — J.K.

Text © 2006 Jessica Scott Kerrin
Illustrations © 2006 Joseph Kelly

This is a work of fiction and any resemblance of characters to persons living or
dead is purely coincidental.

Kids Can Press acknowledges the financial support of the Government of Ontario,
through the Ontario Media Development Corporation's Ontario Book Initiative;
the Ontario Arts Council; the Canada Council for the Arts; and the Government
of Canada, through the BPIDP, for our publishing activity.

Published in Canada by
Kids Can Press Ltd.
29 Birch Avenue
Toronto, ON M4V 1E2

Published in the U.S. by
Kids Can Press Ltd.
2250 Military Road
Tonawanda, NY 14150

www.kidscanpress.com

Edited by Debbie Rogosin
Designed by Julia Naimska
Printed and bound in Canada

The art in this book was drawn with graphite
and charcoal; shading was added digitally.

The text is set in GarthGraphic.

CM 06 0 9 8 7 6 5 4 3 2 1
CM PA 06 0 9 8 7 6 5 4 3 2 1

Library and Archives Canada Cataloguing in Publication

Kerrin, Jessica Scott
    Martin Bridge blazing ahead! / written by Jessica Scott Kerrin ;
illustrated by Joseph Kelly.

ISBN-13: 978-1-55337-961-4 (bound) ISBN-13: 978-1-55337-962-1 (pbk.)
ISBN-10: 1-55337-961-6 (bound) ISBN-10: 1-55337-962-4 (pbk.)

I. Kelly, Joseph II. Title.

PS8621.E77M36 2006   jC813'.6   C2006-901302-0

Kids Can Press is a /@rus™ Entertainment company

Contents

Meet ...

Martin

Trailblazing Junior Badger

Alex

King of pranks

Clark

Houdini with tape

Stuart

Camp maestro

Dad

Leading expert on the use
and abuse of tools

Mom

Family photographer

Head
Badger
Bob

Lost without a compass

Jenny

Mechanical genius

Zip
Rideout

"Ready and steady"

Volt
Thundercloud

Lightning bolt superhero
and toolbox wizard

Relish

"Psssst! Check this out," said Martin's friend Alex from the backseat as he pulled a jar from his knapsack.

Martin turned around to read the label.

"Relish?" he asked. "What do you have relish for?"

"It's not relish," said Alex mysteriously. "Open the lid." He rocked the jar from side to side with a flick of his wrist.

"Forget it!" said Martin matter-of-factly. He straightened the tie of his Junior Badger uniform. Knowing Alex, there could be anything in that jar.

Anything.

And Alex's eagerness made Martin extra suspicious.

Martin returned his attention to the road. His dad was driving, but Head Badger Bob's van led the way. Eight vehicles trailed behind, each one crammed with Junior Badgers going on their very first overnight camp trip.

It was supposed to be a short ride, yet they had been driving for hours. Martin's dad thought Head Badger Bob was lost, especially since they had passed the same gas station twice.

"I'll open it," offered Clark. He and Stuart were sharing a seat with Martin.

Alex handed the jar to him. Martin and Stuart leaned away.

"It's just relish," said Clark with disappointment.

Martin cautiously peered inside the jar at the chunky green contents.

"Try it," urged Alex.

Clark was about to stick his finger in when Stuart batted Clark's hand away.

"I wouldn't if I were you," warned Stuart. He commandeered the jar and twisted around to face Alex. "What is it, really?" he demanded.

"Classic horror-movie slime," announced Alex in a haunted house voice.

"Can you eat it?" asked Clark. He was known for eating anything on a dare. Crayons. Eraser shavings. Even paste.

"Clark!" blurted Martin. "You've really got to stick to regular food. No kidding."

"Come on, Martin," said Alex. "Where's your sense of adventure?" He turned to Clark. "Sure you can eat it," he said. "I made it from stuff in the kitchen. It's all natural."

"Natural slime," Stuart scoffed. "Now I've heard everything."

But Martin had watched a show about different types of slime on the all-science channel.

"Let's have a look," he said with new fascination. He took the jar from Stuart to pour some into his hand.

"Stop!" said Alex. "Don't waste it!" He rescued the jar from Martin.

"What are you going to do with it?" asked Martin.

"You'll see," said Alex. He returned the jar to his knapsack. "I just hope we get there soon. I've got to get this back in a fridge, or it will go bad."

Martin glanced warily at Stuart.

Stuart shook his head. "Ka-boom!" he

muttered. Stuart said "ka-boom" whenever he thought something would go wrong.

A few minutes later, their van passed a large sign.

"Camp Kitchywahoo," read Martin's dad with relief. "Next turn on the right."

The boys shifted excitedly in their seats as Martin's dad parked beside the large ranch-style gate that marked the entrance to the camp.

"We're here!" he announced. The boys whooped and tumbled out the doors as the rest of the cars and vans pulled up.

Martin took a deep breath. The air smelled like pine needles and moss and lake water. This was going to be way better than playing park rangers in his tree fort back home!

"Attention, men!" announced Head Badger Bob between cupped hands. "Grab your gear and follow me!"

The troop formed a ragged line and

marched past the gate into the compound. Shoving through the double doors of the lodge, they gathered in the colossal mess hall. Rows of tables and benches made from logs filled the room. The kitchen was off to one side, and tiny cabin rooms beckoned from the other.

Martin looked up at the banner that hung from the ceiling. "Blazing Ahead," he read out loud. It was the Junior Badger motto.

Head Badger Bob consulted his giant clipboard jammed with papers.

"Listen up!" he ordered above the growing hum of excitement. "Pick your bunks and be quick. We have a busy day ahead of us."

Badgers scurried past him, then crisscrossed from cabin to cabin trying to team up with friends.

"In here, Martin!"

Martin followed Alex's voice to cabin room number seven.

"Saved the top bunk for you," Alex continued in high spirits.

Somehow, Alex had already unpacked. His gear was strewn everywhere. Stuart and

Clark sat on the opposite bunk beds bounce-testing the mattresses. Their room had a soft, woodsy smell, and former Badgers had covered the walls with their signatures.

It was nice.

"Okay, troop!" Head Badger Bob called as he marched up and down the hallway. Papers kept dropping from his clipboard. "I want everyone to report to the flagpole. Pack your bug spray, your field guide and your mess kit."

"What's a messy kit?" asked Alex.

"A *mess* kit," corrected Stuart, side-stepping Alex's overflowing duffle bag. "But I could see how you'd get confused."

Alex scowled.

"A mess kit is your plate and cup and fork," explained Martin proudly. "We're going to have our lunch in the woods."

At the last Junior Badger meeting, the troop had been given a schedule chock-full of meals and activities. Martin had reviewed it every night at bedtime for the past week.

"You go ahead," said Alex. "I've got to put this in fridge." He bolted out the door with his jar.

Martin sighed. He knew that *someone* would be slimed before the weekend was over. But maybe, if he kept an extra-sharp lookout, it wouldn't be him.

The entire troop stood waiting by the flagpole when Alex finally joined them.

"Let's head out!" commanded Head Badger Bob, big whistle, compass and binoculars hanging from his neck.

The troop whooped.

When Martin entered the woods, it felt like he was stepping into a tunnel. The trees overhead blocked much of the sun. The path was damp and spongy.

Pinecones. Birch bark. Deer droppings. Head Badger Bob pointed them all out. And the Badgers made notes in their field guides to earn their Junior Hiking Badge.

Martin was about to draw the woodpecker he had glimpsed when Alex came over.

"Look what I spotted," he said mischievously. He had drawn some kind of life form in the margin. It had knobby antennae, an extra set of arms and it appeared to be yelling.

Martin gave him a puzzled look.

"It's Stuart," said Alex, chuckling, and then he moved off.

When Martin looked up again, Alex was showing his sketch to Stuart. The shoving match that followed broke up only when Head Badger Bob blasted his whistle.

Birds and animals scrambled for cover, and any chance of seeing more wildlife disappeared with them.

At last, the troop came to a clearing and stopped for lunch.

"The blackflies seem hungry, too," observed Martin, swatting his neck. He doused himself with half a bottle of bug spray.

Satisfied with his efforts, Martin turned to Alex, who was sitting beside him. Only Alex was now fiddling with Martin's mess kit!

"Gotcha!" Martin shouted as he snatched his mess kit back.

"Got me? For what?" asked Alex, startled.

"What were you doing with my mess kit?" Martin demanded, checking for slime.

"*Your* mess kit? That's *mine*."

"Oh, *really*?" said Martin, eyebrow raised. He flipped the kit over and pointed to his name written on the bottom.

"Easy mistake," said Alex. "My mess kit's the same color." He looked about. "Oh. Here's mine." He plucked his kit from the ground nearby.

Martin stared at the two mess kits. They *were* the same color.

"Fine," admitted Martin, wagging his finger. "But I'm on to you."

Alex shrugged innocently. His infuriating grin said something else.

The hike back was uneventful except for

the occasional soaker that happened
whenever a Badger stepped in a
puddle deeper than he thought.

"Cripes!" muttered Martin when he
got one, too. He had been so busy keeping
an eye on Alex, he hadn't watched
where he was going. His footsteps made
embarrassingly squishy sounds all the
way back to the lodge, much to Alex's
amusement.

After a big dinner of spaghetti, with chocolate brownies for dessert, the troop was ready for the next adventure.

"Attention, men!" Head Badger Bob called as they cleared their plates. "It's time for a campfire. Go back to your rooms and grab your jackets."

Benches scraped against the floor as the mess hall quickly emptied.

"How's it going, Sport?" asked Martin's dad as he intercepted Martin.

"Great, Dad," said Martin, anxiously watching Alex bolt from the room at top speed. "But I should get to my cabin."

"Oh, yes. Campfire," said his dad appreciatively.

Martin nodded, even though the campfire was *not* his immediate concern.

"See you out there," called his dad as Martin hurried away.

Martin barely heard him. He burst through the doorway and saw Alex scrambling up to Martin's bunk.

"Gotcha this time!" shouted Martin.

"Got me?" repeated Alex, puzzled. He turned around on the ladder to face Martin. "For what?"

"Get away from my bunk!"

"I wasn't doing anything to your bunk. I was juggling," said Alex, pointing to a couple of pinecones on the floor. "But I lost control."

"Move out of my way," insisted Martin, pushing by Alex. He whipped open his sleeping bag.

No slime.

He thrust his hand under his pillow.

Nothing!

But he did find the third pinecone
wedged in the corner of his bunk.

"Here," he said curtly, handing it to Alex.

"You seem awfully jumpy," said Alex in
a tone that made Martin's ears burn.

Moments later, smoke began to drift back to the lodge. Cabin rooms sprang to life as Badgers rummaged through their duffle bags for their jackets, then scrambled out the door.

Martin stayed behind, searching for his Park Ranger Super-Charged All-Night Flashlight. He finally found it buried underneath Alex's jumbled gear. Cripes! Martin rushed outside and joined the others.

Flames crackled and licked the tepee of logs under a black

28

sky loaded with stars. The campfire blazed so high, the troop had to stand way back.

Martin glanced over at his dad and the other leaders, who stood by with buckets of water. Head Badger Bob busily whittled marshmallow sticks, ignoring the raging inferno.

Eventually, the fire burned down. Head
Badger Bob showed them how
to roast marshmallows
and slide them between
chocolate chip cookies. It
made for a delicious, gooey sandwich.

Martin ate six.

"Okay, troop," boomed Head Badger
Bob. "A few of you are going for your Junior
Campfire Badge tonight. To earn this badge,
you have to entertain the troop."

There were excited murmurs from the
crowd.

"First up," said Head Badger Bob,
consulting his clipboard, "is Stuart. Stuart
is going to play the recorder."

Stuart stood. He
played a soulful
rendition of *Row,
Row, Row Your Boat*
while Alex hummed
loudly, off-key. Stuart
glowered at him until
Alex stopped. Then
Stuart played the first

few bars of the national anthem for good measure.

He received a polite round of applause.

"Next up," announced Head Badger Bob, "is Clark. Clark will wow us with some magic."

Clark stood and pulled a roll of tape from his pocket. "Name an object, any object," he called out.

"Clouds!" Alex shouted a split second before the others.

Clark blinked at him. "Pick something more solid," he urged.

"Campfire!" Alex called out. "Lake!"

"Solid!" insisted Clark. "With shape!"

"Bunk beds," Martin suggested, coming to Clark's rescue.

"Thank you," said Clark with relief.

"Bunk beds it is." He turned his back on the circle and began to fiddle with the tape.

Screech, scritch went the tape as he pulled off various lengths. After a few short minutes, Clark wheeled around and held out his hand. There in his palm was a dollhouse-sized bunk bed made entirely out of tape. With his other hand, he placed two tiny campers on the bunks and tucked them in with all-tape blankets.

"Ooooooh!" chimed the crowd, applauding earnestly. "Neat trick!"

"Martin Bridge," called Head Badger Bob. "You're next. Martin will entertain us with a lesson on Morse code."

Martin stood and turned on his flashlight.
"Morse code is a way to send messages
without a phone or a computer," explained
Martin. "Each letter is made up of short
and long bursts of light or sound. I can
signal any letter you want."

"How about the letter I'm supposed to write to my mom on this trip," Alex called out. "Can you signal that?"

"Not letters you mail," said Martin, rolling his eyes. "Letters of the alphabet."

He took a deep breath, refusing to let Alex rattle him. "Here's how to signal the word 'lost.'"

Martin proceeded to flash his light on and off, naming the letters as he signaled.

"Now see if you can guess *this* word. It uses most of the letters in 'lost.'"

Martin flashed "stop." But guesses from the troop were drowned out by Alex.

"Clouds!" he shouted above the others. "Campfire! Lake!"

"No," said Martin, shooting Alex an icy glare. "I spelled 'stop.' Now here's one more for you to guess. It uses some of the letters in 'lost' and 'stop.'"

Martin flashed his light for three short bursts, three long ones, then three short.

This time, the troop buzzed with anticipation. Even Alex.

"I signaled 'S-O-S.' It stands for 'save our souls,'" said Martin. "That means 'send help' if you're in an emergency."

Martin received a hearty round of applause. His dad gave him the thumbs-up.

"We have two more entertainers tonight," announced Head Badger Bob. "Next up is Jonathan. Jonathan is going to lead us in a song about —" He checked his clipboard. "— swallowing a fly."

Martin's dad leaned over and spoke quietly. "Jonathan got homesick, remember?

His mom came to pick him up an hour ago."

The troop nodded sadly.

"Right," said Head Badger Bob. "Well, then. Last up is Alex. Alex, I believe you have a story to tell?"

"I do!" Alex jumped up with a wicked smile.

Before Alex even started, Martin flashed "S-O-S." Stuart threw his arms up in the air and mouthed, "Ka-boom." Clark joined the fun by jabbing relentlessly at the fire with his marshmallow stick until sparks shot up.

Ignoring their antics, Alex launched into a story about a space alien who was posing as a Junior Badger on a camping trip.

He went on at length about how the campers went missing, one by one, whenever they ventured into the woods. Even the leaders disappeared. Only puddles remained where they had last been seen. As if they had *melted*!

At last, there were only two campers left. And it was getting dark.

"They made each other promise not to leave the lodge until help

arrived," said Alex solemnly.

The circle of Badgers leaned forward, but nobody spoke.

"And to be sure, they shook hands on it," said Alex. He reached out to shake Martin's hand.

Playing along, Martin shook, but Alex didn't let go.

"And then do you know what happened?" asked Alex mysteriously.

Martin gave a small shrug.

Alex measured out his next words carefully. "One of the campers looked at the other and said ... 'Gotcha!!'"

Alex pulled away from Martin dramatically. Long strands of chunky slime stretched between their hands.

Some of the younger Badgers screamed.

"Good one," muttered Martin, wiping his hand on his jacket. He slipped Alex a smile.

The troop gave them both a standing ovation.

After that, the Badgers went back to roasting marshmallows. Martin had never been so full in all his life. It almost hurt. But he managed to force down three more.

Now that Alex's prank was over, Martin could relax.

Still …

It would be fun to get Alex back.

But how?

Lost in thought, he reached for another marshmallow.

The full moon was beaming directly overhead when Head Badger Bob finally announced, "Let's put this fire to rest."

They doused the flames and trekked back to the lodge.

After changing into his park ranger pajamas, Martin clambered to the top bunk and slid into his sleeping bag. He could feel the bunks shake as Alex climbed in below.

"Hey, Alex!" Martin called out in the dark. "I'm going to get you back."

"Fat chance," Alex taunted. *"I'm* the king of pranks. If there was a badge for pranks, I'd get it. And besides, I still have plenty more slime in the fridge."

Martin leaned over the rails to look down at Alex. Alex stared back, an impish grin on his moonlit face.

Martin rolled onto his side and
schemed earnestly until he fell asleep.
The next morning he woke up with a plan.
Martin smiled smugly. All he had to do
now was get a little help.

After an enormous pancake breakfast,
everyone was fitted with life jackets, and
the troop headed down to the lake for

canoe lessons. Alex paired with Stuart,
leaving Martin with Clark.

Perfect!

Martin climbed into the stern of a
canoe, and Clark sat in the bow. Once they
got good at paddling together *and* in the
same direction, Martin leaned forward.

"Hey, Clark," he whispered. "Want to
help me play a
trick on Alex?"

Just then, Alex
glided by and
splashed them with
his paddle before
quickly slipping
out of range.

"You bet I do!"
exclaimed Clark,

shaking the water from his hair. "His campfire suggestions were awful."

"Good," said Martin, lifting his feet out of the puddle on the bottom of the canoe. "I've signed us up to help with lunch. It's part of my plan."

Campers earned Junior Helping Hand Badges if they assisted with one of the meals.

"But we'll have to leave canoeing early," said Clark, a note of disappointment in his voice.

"It'll be worth it," said Martin. "Trust me." He proceeded to whisper his entire plan so there would be no chance of Alex overhearing.

"Brilliant," said Clark enthusiastically.

They paddled around the lake once more and then returned to the dock.

"We're going to help with lunch," said
Martin to his dad as he helped them bail
out the water.

After they tended to the canoe, Martin
traipsed back to the lodge with all-too-
familiar squishy footsteps. Only this time,
both shoes were squelching.
So were Clark's.

"Double cripes," Martin muttered.

They changed into dry shoes, then beelined it to the kitchen. Head Badger Bob stood in front of a huge pot of water, dumping all the hot dogs in at once.

"Reporting for duty," said Martin, cautiously eyeing the overfilled pot. "What would you like us to do?"

"You can haul out the dishes and cutlery," ordered Head Badger Bob.

"What about ketchup and relish?" asked Martin helpfully. "Can we set them out, too?"

Head Badger Bob waved away the billowing steam with his tongs. Then the pot began to boil over.

"Sure," he agreed quickly, distracted by the ensuing mess.

"Okay," Martin whispered to Clark. "We haven't got much time. You grab the dishes. I'll go find Alex's jar of relish and make sure it ends up at our table."

"And Alex will spread it on his hot dog!" exclaimed Clark gleefully, repeating what Martin had told him in the canoe.

Martin beamed. "Now, fall out," he said, Head Badger Bob–style.

Martin made his way to the fridge and yanked open the door.

Whoa! It was jam-packed.

He began to pull out the items one by one.

Milk. Apple juice. Lettuce. Carrots. Broccoli. *Broccoli?* It was untouched. Must have been Martin's mom who sent it. Martin shoved the broccoli way to the back. Ham. Cheese. More milk. Chocolate chips. He took a big handful. Ketchup. Mustard ...

But no relish!

Where could it be?! Martin began to panic. He quickly pulled out everything else holus-bolus.

"Three short bursts, three long, three short!!" shouted Clark.

Martin wheeled around to see his dad striding toward him. Martin glanced at the pile of groceries at his feet.

"What are you doing, Sport?" asked his dad. There was an edge to his voice.

"Helping with lunch," said Martin meekly.

"More like helping yourself *to* lunch," said his dad. Then he added, "Where's the chocolate?"

Martin wiped his mouth guiltily, then rooted around and pulled out the bag of chocolate chips. His dad took a handful.

"Why don't you go help Clark?"

"But —"

"Go on," insisted his dad.

Martin watched helplessly as his dad took another handful, then started to repack the food. It would have felt so good to see Alex eat his own nasty relish! If only —

"Still here?" asked his dad coolly, turning around.

Martin sagged in defeat and joined an equally disappointed Clark in the mess hall.

They were setting out the last stacks of plates when the troop began to tumble through the doors.

Head Badger Bob

bustled in from the kitchen carrying two large trays.

"Attention, men!" he announced. "I've already dressed the hot dogs. These ones have ketchup only." He held up a tray. "And these ones have the works." He held up a second tray.

"That reminds me," said Alex, who stood nearby. He dashed up behind Head Badger Bob and snatched a hot dog from the tray with the works before disappearing into the kitchen.

Head Badger Bob didn't notice. He set the trays on the food table beside the bowls of salad and potato chips and the stacks of plates.

"Start the line here." He pointed. "And make sure you fill up. It's a long ride home."

Badgers rushed to the table. Everyone talked at once, but the mess hall gradually grew quiet as the troop filled their plates and sat down.

Clark handed Martin a hot dog when they got to the trays.

"Here you go," he said. "The works."

Martin reached for it just as Alex burst into the mess hall.

"Has anybody seen my slime?!" he called frantically. "I had it in a relish jar!"

The line came to a halt. Those seated stopped eating, their hot dogs frozen in midair.

Head Badger Bob cleared his throat. "Where was the jar?" he asked. For once, his voice wasn't booming.

"In the fridge door," said Alex.

Head Badger Bob let out a small gasp.

The mess hall full of Badgers stared in growing alarm at Head Badger Bob, then at the tray with the works, then at Alex and the half-eaten hot dog in his hand.

Alex gulped.

"The works?" repeated Martin to a jubilant Clark.

"I'll pass," he said with relish.

Lightning Bolts

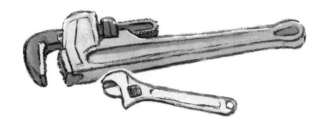

Martin was watching his favorite show, *Zip Rideout: Space Cadet,* when he saw smoke wafting outside the window, then heard shouting.

Martin was not alarmed. He merely turned up the volume, determined to watch *Zip* to the very end.

"Martin," interrupted his mom from the doorway. "Your dad's calling you."

"Now?" asked Martin, sinking farther into the sofa.

"Yes, now," said his mom in her no-fooling-around voice. "Please go see what he wants." She turned on her heel.

 "I *know* what he wants," muttered Martin. He sighed as he clicked off his show, then stared at the blank screen, wishing he were at Alex's or Stuart's house. He was sure his best friends would be watching their space hero without *any* interruptions.

"Martin!" called his dad from outside the window as he tapped the glass with his ring finger.

"Okay, okay," said Martin with resignation. He trundled outside and joined his dad.

There in the middle of the yard sat their dilapidated lawn mower.

Martin *hated* that lawn mower more than anything.

More than running out of Zip Rideout Space Flakes at breakfast.

More than his school bus driver's cranky-pants comments.

Even more than his mom's spring cleaning regimen.

"You know the drill," said Martin's dad. "Grab hold of Laverne for me."

Martin's dad had named the lawn mower Laverne after an old aunt of his. Aunt Laverne only did things when she wanted to. Her voice sounded all rusty. And she had blue hair the color of lawn mower smoke.

Even worse, Aunt Laverne always seemed to be wagging her knobby finger at Martin whenever she came for a visit.

Aunt Laverne was not his favorite family member.

Martin steadied the lawn mower by grasping the handlebar while his dad yanked the pull-cord again and again. Martin had to hold firm because the lawn mower had lost its fourth wheel some time ago.

Probably before I was born, thought Martin.

The lawn mower sputtered and hiccupped more smoke. *Ka-fump-fump-fump.* *Ka-fump-fump-fump.* But it refused to start.

"Wheel Laverne onto the driveway," said Martin's dad enthusiastically, "so we can have a better look."

Frowning, Martin dragged the lawn mower across the partially cut grass while his dad scooted into the garage. Out came the toolbox.

Martin groaned.

"Can I go in now, Dad?" he asked, dumping the

lawn mower onto the pavement. *"Zip's* on."

"Zip's always on," said his dad, flipping the lawn mower onto its side. "And besides, Sport, I need your help with the tools. Hand me the crescent wrench, please."

Martin sighed and shuffled over to the
toolbox. He flipped open the lid. Inside was
an assorted mess of tools.

 Wrenches, metal
files, screwdrivers.
Ratchets, hammers,
staple gun.
Martin dug around
until he spotted the two-fingered claw with
the twirling spool. It had dents from when
Martin had used it to nail up his "Keep
Out" tree fort sign. Martin remembered
how his dad had bolted across the lawn
and delivered his very first lecture on Tools
and Their Use and Abuse.

"Here, Dad," said Martin, handing the
wrench to him handle first, the way he'd
been taught. Then he added, "I was

watching the one where Zip discovers a
system of dwarf stars."

"Dwarf stars. Haven't you already seen
that episode?" asked his dad, pulling off the
carburetor.

"Not lately," grumbled Martin.

"Hand me the needle-nose
pliers, Sport," said his dad,
a smudge of grease on his
cheek. He was fiddling
with the spark plug.

Martin rooted around for the tool that looked like the beak of a pterodactyl. He had used the pliers once to punch air holes into the lid of a jam jar for his butterfly collection. That, too, was a no-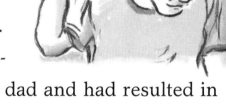
no according to his dad and had resulted in another Use and Abuse lecture.

Martin tried a new tack.

"Didn't *you* have a favorite superhero when you were a kid?" he asked grumpily, handing his dad the pliers.

"I sure did," came his dad's surprise response. "Mine was a comic book hero named Volt Thundercloud. He could shoot electricity from his fingertips. He was unstoppable."

"Volt Thundercloud," repeated Martin, intrigued. For a moment, he forgot his annoyance over missing his show. "What did Volt look like?"

"He wore an all-black disguise. Black cape. Black mask. Oh, and lightning bolts that blazed up and down his arms." Martin's dad paused. "I haven't thought about him in years."

"Lightning bolts?" repeated Martin. "And did Volt fight evil, too?"

"You bet," said Martin's dad. "Volt was very resourceful. He would get out of danger by using ordinary things in ingenious ways. And there was always a terrific section in the comic called 'Did you know,' where Volt would teach us about tools and gadgets and how to fix things."

"Like lawn mowers?" said Martin dryly.

"Very funny, Sport," said Martin's dad, turning back to the lawn mower. "We all wanted to be like Volt. Pass me the screwdriver, please."

"Which type, Dad? Cross or slot head?"

"Phillips." His dad stood and smiled. This was a test.

Martin had to think a minute, and then he remembered. Phillips screwdrivers had cross heads. And they were not to be used to mix paint. His dad had caught Martin doing that once when he was working on one of his rockets. Martin dug out the Phillips, its handle still stained with flecks of fireball red.

The heat of the afternoon sun was making the back of Martin's neck sweat.

"Why don't we just buy a new lawn mower?" he complained while tugging at his sticky shirt. "This thing never works."

"Oh, we can't give up on Laverne that easily," said Martin's dad. "As Volt Thundercloud would say, all she needs is some tweaking now and then."

He flipped the lawn mower onto its three wheels. Martin automatically clutched the handlebar as his dad yanked the pull-cord. The lawn mower wheezed to an unconvincing start. *Ka-fum-fum-fum-fum* ...

"See?" said his dad jovially, waving off the cloud of blue smoke while Martin doubled over gasping for air. It was worse than choking on Aunt Laverne's lavender perfume.

"How are my boys doing?" called Martin's mom as she came out of the house, screen door snapping behind her.

She handed them each a glass of lemonade. They gathered around the shimmying lawn mower, Martin's dad beaming in triumph.

But that proved to be too much attention for the lawn mower. As if for

spite, it sputtered, then died.

Nobody said anything for a moment. Then Martin took a loud slurp.

"Can I go in now?" he asked, crunching down on an ice cube. Perhaps there was still time to catch the tail end of his show.

He looked imploringly at his mom, who nodded slightly, then whispered something to his dad.

"Sure, Sport," said Martin's dad, a touch of sadness in his voice. "I guess I can handle Laverne from here."

Without waiting for his dad to finish, Martin dashed inside, flopped onto the sofa and clicked on his show.

Too late. The end credits were already rolling up the screen.

Cripes!

The next afternoon, exactly the same thing happened, just as Zip's rocket blasted across the Milky Way. The devious lawn mower coughed up blue smoke and refused to continue, followed by the predictable tapping on the window.

"Pass me the crescent wrench, Sport," said his dad, who stooped over the upturned lawn mower while Martin fumed.

All around, the air buzzed with sounds of neighbors cutting *their* lawns in lickety-split time.

Martin's mom came out with two more glasses of lemonade, then snapped a photograph of the two of them working in

the driveway. Martin refused to uncross his arms for the picture. And he intensified his scowl.

After what felt like an eternity of tweaking to Martin, his dad confessed that he couldn't get the lawn mower started at all. Not even a single *ka-fump*. One by one, he dropped tools into the box and snapped the lid shut with a sigh.

Martin was not sympathetic. Today's infuriating attempts at coaxing the lawn mower to start had taken so long, he didn't even get to watch the *Zip Rideout* end credits!

That night, Martin dreamt he pushed the hateful lawn mower off a mammoth cliff that overlooked the city's garbage dump. It somersaulted in the air before smashing onto the trash heap, tires ricocheting in three directions.

Martin woke up with a smile. He slid down the railing in his rocket-covered pajamas and fixed himself his usual bowl of Zip Rideout Space Flakes. His mom was reading the newspaper at the table when his dad came in to get some coffee.

"Here's an interesting ad," she said, pointing to the newspaper. "Announcing the grand opening of Mighty's Small Engine Repair. Specializing in snowblowers, outboards, motorcycles and, look here, *lawn mowers.*"

"Really?" said Martin's dad. "Where is it?"

"Victoria Road just past Fenwick." She looked up. "Hey, that's not far. Why don't you take the lawn mower there?"

"What do you say, Martin?" asked his dad, new hope in his voice. "Maybe we should give Laverne one last chance."

"Ready and steady," said Martin, sounding like Zip Rideout on the final leg of a mission. He was sure that an actual mechanic would take one look at their rusty, three-wheeled smoke trap and insist that his dad buy a new one. Then Martin's days of missing *Zip Rideout* would finally be over.

They lifted the lawn mower into the back of the van, Martin heaving his side as if he was turfing a garbage bag into the bin.

"Easy there, Sport," said his dad. "Be gentle."

For the first few blocks, Laverne's obnoxious stench of burnt oil and rotting grass clippings filled the van, forcing them to open their windows. Martin gulped the fresh air. He couldn't figure out why his dad was going to such great lengths to save something so old and crotchety.

Not just great lengths. Super heroic lengths!

"Victoria Road just past Fenwick," said Martin's dad. "This must be it."

He pulled into the parking lot. Over the front door of the new garage hung a brightly painted sign that announced "Mighty's Small Engine Repair." It had a bulldog hefting an engine over its head. They pushed the door open and went inside.

"Can I help you?" asked the clerk enthusiastically from behind the counter.

"Yes," said Martin's dad. "Our lawn mower needs repair."

"And we'd like someone here to check it out," said Martin, blazing ahead. "A mechanic," he added. "Someone who knows about engines," he said for good measure.

"I think we can help you," said the clerk. "Have a seat. I'll see who's free." She disappeared behind the repair shop door.

Martin studied the lobby. Because it was so new, there were no grease spots on the floor and no cracked vinyl benches with stuffing poking out. But loudspeakers blared heavy metal music, and he saw familiar advertisements for mechanical parts on the walls. Martin nodded, satisfied that real mechanics worked here.

"Martin? Martin Bridge?"

Startled, Martin turned to see who was calling him.

"Jenny?" he said in surprise.

There stood Jenny, his one-time substitute school bus driver. The world's best, in fact. But then his old driver had come back. Martin had not seen Jenny since.

Jenny was wearing coveralls with the Mighty's bulldog and her name stitched on the shoulder.

"Do you work here?" Martin asked.

"Just started!" said Jenny, beaming. She

reached over to shake his dad's hand. "I'm
Jenny. And you must be Mr. Bridge."

"Nice to meet you," said Martin's dad.

"You have a terrific boy," said Jenny. "A
big Zip Rideout fan. Member of the Junior
Badgers. And very artistic, as I recall."

Martin's ears turned red. "We're here

about our lawn mower," he said, shrugging modestly, but enjoying her compliment.

"Let's have a look," said Jenny brightly.

They headed outside, and Martin helped his dad unload the lawn mower from the van. To show Jenny just what he thought of their lawn mower, Martin dropped his side to the pavement.

"Careful, Martin!" his dad implored.

Rust flakes sprinkled the ground at Martin's feet like a caustic scolding.

"Wow," said Jenny, circling the relic. "This is a real old-timer."

Martin's heart lifted. "Too old to fix. Right, Jenny?"

"Oh, I'm not saying that. This model can last years."

"It's already *been* years," said Martin,

smile fading. "And look how rusty it is. There's hardly any paint left. Don't you think we need a new one?" he added meekly.

"Not necessarily," said Jenny, crouching down. "I've seen some of these mowers go forever with the right tweaking here and there."

"Well, now!" said his dad, giving Martin's back a pat. "That's just what Volt Thundercloud would say!"

"I remember Volt Thundercloud!" exclaimed Jenny. "He was that lightning bolt superhero who fixed things!"

The mention of Volt sparked Jenny's enthusiasm to new heights.

"Can you leave it with me for a few days?" she asked. "I might even be able to track down a fourth wheel for you."

Martin's hope for a new lawn mower went up in smoke.

Blue smoke.

"Wonderful!" said his dad, winking at Martin.

Martin did not wink back. And he barely said good-bye to Jenny as he climbed into the van.

But Martin did manage one happy thought. While the cantankerous lawn mower was in the shop, he would be able to watch his show with *no* interruptions.

Days drifted by, the grass grew longer and the garage began to smell fresher. Then

one afternoon, Alex and Stuart came over on their bikes. The boys gathered in Martin's driveway.

"Did you see *Zip* yesterday?" asked Stuart. "When he flew through the exploding yellow nebula?"

"You bet! The whole thing!" said Martin proudly.

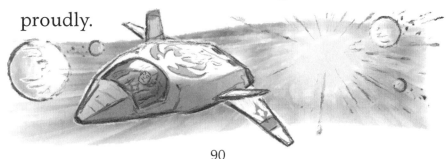

"Hey, my seat's loose," said Alex, climbing off his bike. His little brother was always borrowing Alex's wheels and crashing into things.

"That's easy to fix," said Martin. "Grab my dad's crescent wrench. It's in the toolbox in the garage."

"The crescent what?" asked Alex.

"The crescent wrench," repeated Martin.

Alex and Stuart stared at him blankly.

"I'll get it," said Martin, passing Alex's bike back to him.

He retrieved the wrench and handed it to Alex. "Here you go," he said.

Alex held it as if Martin had just handed him a high-tech gadget designed to fix rocket boosters. Shrugging, he started to

hammer the wrench against his bike seat.

"Whoa, there!" said Martin, grabbing
the wrench back. He tightened the seat bolt
while giving a mini version of his dad's
lecture on Tools and Their Use and Abuse.
His friends looked on in awe.

"Say, Martin," said Stuart. "My bell's loose. Think you can fix that, too?"

"Just needs a tweak," said Martin over his shoulder as he headed back to the garage. He came out wielding a slot head screwdriver and deftly secured the bell.

The boys spent the rest of the afternoon touring the neighborhood before rushing back to Martin's house for their show.

The dreaded call came the very next day.

Martin picked up the telephone thinking it might be Alex, who had left his Zip Rideout goggles behind.

"Hello?" said Martin.

"Hi, Martin. This is Jenny. Your lawn mower's ready."

"I'll let Dad know," said Martin coldly. He hung up and let out a long, frustrated sigh. Couldn't Jenny tell he didn't *want* that lawn mower back?!

Martin traipsed outside. The garage door was open, but he dawdled in the yard. Then it occurred to him that if he hurried, they could get the lawn mower back home in time for his show.

He popped his head into the garage. His dad was pinning the photograph of them

working on the lawn mower to the wall
behind his cluttered workbench.

Martin stood perplexed. He knew his
dad only put up pictures of things he really
liked. There were a couple of Martin's
drawings of Zip Rideout, magazine pictures
of sports cars and some aerial photographs

from the helicopter his dad sometimes got to ride in at work.

Martin was about to ask why that loathsome piece of junk should make the wall when his dad interrupted.

"What's up?" he asked.

"The lawn mower's ready," said Martin glumly.

"That's great, Sport!!" exclaimed his dad, taking a step back to admire his wall collage. "Grab my keys in the kitchen, and we'll go get Laverne."

When they entered the lobby

of Mighty's Small Engine Repair, Martin
went straight for the clerk.

"Our lawn mower's ready," he declared,
leaning with both hands on the counter. *Zip*
was on in less than an hour.

"I'll see if Jenny's free," said the clerk,
and she disappeared behind the repair
shop door.

Standing there, Martin returned his thoughts to his dad and why saving the lawn mower mattered so much. It was a puzzle.

"Martin!" said Jenny as she pushed through the door. "And Mr. Bridge! How *are* you?"

"Good, thanks!" said Martin's dad, shaking her hand vigorously.

"I have a surprise for you," said Jenny. "Follow me."

They entered the repair shop and stopped. There in the center was a lawn mower. Only it wasn't the lawn mower in the photograph that Martin's dad had pinned to his workbench wall. This one looked brand new.

"Oh, my," said Martin's dad, taking a small step forward. "You *painted* it?"

"Sure did," said Jenny proudly. "Do you like it, Martin?"

Martin gulped hard. Cripes! Now their lawn mower looked as if it would outlast dwarf stars!

"It's not quite done," said Jenny, misreading Martin's expression. "I was going to add some decals to the sides. But then I remembered how artistic you are, so I thought *you'd* like to pick out a design."

"Maybe flames like Zip Rideout's rocket," suggested Martin's dad eagerly. "What do you say, Martin?"

Martin knew he had to say something. Jenny had gone to so much trouble.

"It's beautiful," he mustered.

Martin's dad returned to the lobby to pay the bill. Martin remained behind, staring at their lawn mower with its gorgeous new paint job.

"Martin?" Jenny hunkered down beside him. "Is something wrong?" she asked.

"It's just that ..." Martin faltered. "Well. I didn't really want this lawn mower back."

"Oh. I thought you'd change your mind once I fixed it up," she said.

Martin sighed. "You don't understand. My friends get to watch *Zip Rideout* whenever they want. But every

time *this* breaks —" He paused to kick the
new tire. "— I miss
my show."

"Why's that?"

"Because my dad
wants me to help him fix it."

"He does?" asked Jenny in awe. "Wow! I
wish my dad had fixed stuff with me when
I was a kid. I had to learn about mechanics
on my own."

Martin didn't say anything, but he
flashed back to the photograph of him
and his dad with the lawn mower. He
picked up a crescent wrench from Jenny's
workbench and twirled the spool. More
pictures blazed by as he remembered all
the times his dad had taught him about
tools and gadgets and how to fix things.

Then it hit Martin like a bolt of lightning. Volt Thundercloud also taught about tools and gadgets and how to fix things. Just like his dad!

And just like me, thought Martin, proudly recalling his bike repairs.

Martin smiled.

"So what about some decals?" asked Jenny. "Do you want flames?"

"No. Not flames," said Martin, lowering his voice and setting down the tool.

"But I thought you liked Zip Rideout," said Jenny.

"I do," said Martin softly. "But I want something that reminds me of my dad."

"Wonderful! And what would that be?"

"Can you keep a secret?" he asked.

"Sure I can," she whispered back.

Martin told her under his breath. Jenny stood and gave him the thumbs-up.

"Dad," asked Martin when they rejoined

him in the lobby. "Do you think I could stay and help Jenny add a few decals?"

"Sure, Sport," said Martin's dad. He did not catch the knowing glance between Martin and Jenny. "When should I come back to pick you up?"

"An hour," suggested Jenny. "Maybe a bit longer."

His dad checked his watch. "But Martin. You'll miss *Zip*."

Martin shrugged. "Laverne needs a few more tweaks," he said, calling the lawn mower by name for the very first time. "And besides," he continued, "*Zip*'s always on."

Martin walked his dad to the van.

"Ready and steady," said Martin, giving his dad a Zip Rideout salute as the van drove off. His stomach did happy flip-flops, so perfect was his plan.

"Lightning bolts," he had whispered to Jenny.

"Lightning bolts!" exclaimed his dad, hugging Martin tightly when he returned.

"Get the camera!" Martin called to his mom as he and his dad gently lowered Laverne onto the driveway back home.

Make Martin's Slime

WITHDRAWN

Alex won't reveal the formula for his horror-movie slime. But here's a recipe for you to try. Martin saw it on the all-science channel.

* 15 green gummy bears
* 1 300 mL (14 oz.) can *sweetened* condensed milk
* 15 mL (1 tbsp.) cornstarch
* green and blue food coloring

Ask an adult to help you use the stove.

Chop gummy bears into relish-sized pieces. Set aside. Pour milk into a saucepan. Stir in cornstarch. Heat on very low, stirring constantly, until slime thickens slightly (about 10 minutes). Remove from heat. Add food coloring until desired shade of green is reached: 10–20 drops of green and 5–15 drops of blue. Stir well. Let cool. Add gummy bears. The slime will get thick and stretchy as it cools.

When no one is looking, scoop a spoonful into your right palm. Now go find someone to shake hands with, Camp Kitchywahoo–style.

This slime is sticky! When you're done, scrape it into the garbage.

Send Secret Signals

Martin taught the Junior Badgers how to send messages using International Morse code. You can do it, too! Each letter is made up of dots and dashes. For a dot, make a short blink with your flashlight. For a dash, make a long blink.

A	•—	H	••••	N	—•	U	••—
B	—•••	I	••	O	———	V	•••—
C	—•—•	J	•———	P	•——•	W	•——
D	—••	K	—•—	Q	——•—	X	—••—
E	•	L	•—••	R	•—•	Y	—•——
F	••—•	M	——	S	•••	Z	——••
G	——•			T	—		

Can you break the code and answer these questions? Letters are separated by /; words are separated by //.

* What does Martin get in the woods?

  •—//•••/— — —/•—/—•—/•/•—•

* What does Alex say to Martin at the campfire?

  — —•/— — —/—/•—•/••••/•—

* What does Martin like on his hot dogs?

  —/••••/•/•//•— —/— — —/•—•/—•—/•••

Now send some secret signals of your own!

109

Answers: A soaker. Gotcha. The works.

Jessica Scott Kerrin lives in Halifax, Nova Scotia. She earned very few wilderness badges in her day, but she enjoyed roasting marshmallows and relished telling stories around a blazing campfire. Later, her boys taught her more than she ever wanted to know about slime. Yuck! Martin's Slime is their favorite.

Joseph Kelly lives in the Valley of the Moon in Sonoma County, California. In winter, the valley comes alive with millions of red-legged frogs. In summer, mobs of crimson-headed vultures sunbathe behind his home. Joseph sees all this and more when he's not drawing the pictures for the Martin books, which so far have filled up over six hundred notebook pages!

Martin Bridge Ready for Takeoff!

Ka-Boom!

It was Martin's idea to decorate the model rocket with flames. So why did his best friend steal the idea? Now Martin has to come up with something even better in time for Saturday's launch. But will he lose a friend in the process?

Don't miss Martin's first book of adventures, in which his plans for a brilliant rocket, a substitute bus driver and a very old hamster go terribly wrong.

Written by Jessica Scott Kerrin
Illustrated by Joseph Kelly

HC ISBN-13: 978-1-55337-688-0
PB ISBN-13: 978-1-55337-772-6

Martin Bridge On the Lookout!

oh, no!

Martin is all set for a field trip to the dinosaur exhibit at the museum when the bus leaves without him! Now he has to suffer through the day in a junior class and sit beside a boy who eats erasers. Will Martin lose his appetite for adventure?

In this second lively book of illustrated stories, Martin Bridge is on the lookout — for sandwiches made with eraser shavings, for an escaped parakeet and for a Park Ranger Super-Charged All-Night Flashlight.

Written by Jessica Scott Kerrin
Illustrated by Joseph Kelly

HC ISBN-13: 978-1-55337-689-7
PB ISBN-13: 978-1-55337-773-3